HUGA HUGA HIPPO

BOOK 4

The Homecoming - A Hero

BRENDA C. MERCHANT

To order additional copies of this book, contact:
Xlibris
1-888-795-4274
www.Xlibris.com
Orders@Xlibris.com

HUGA HUGA HIPPO

BOOK 4

CHAPTER 1: BAD TIGER MEETS CRANKY CROCK

As a big thunderstorm began to move its rage away from Rivers' Pond, the high winds died to slower gusts and the sound of the thunder and lightning softened to a rumble in the distance. Still, the rain persisted and came down heavy.

Hug arrived at the mud bog. The search party had already been there, so, no one was around. Hug went into the bog to think about how he could be accepted by everyone at Rivers' Pond. Then, he recalled the teachings of his parents and realized that he had been disrespectful, unclean and had just ignored them. Finally, he decided to prove, once and for all, that he could change for the better and be more grown up. He had it! He began to jump around and shout out the words. "I WILL be respectful! I WILL be clean and tidy! I WILL make my family and friends proud!"

Hug dove into the large pond with a SPLASH! He swam, dove, played and quickly rolled in the pond many times, determined to clean the dried mud from his skin. Each time he came out of the pond, he quickly turned and lunged right back into it with a SPLASH! Hug enjoyed his cleaning method and didn't mind the heavy rain. Actually, the heavy rain helped his efforts! Without the mud glued to his body, Hug would no longer have a disgusting stench and, no longer could he be called a dripping blob! His skin color even changed from a dark mud brown to a light grayish brown with a pink underbelly.

Suddenly startled by the sound of a huge SPLASH, Hug quickly came out of the pond and discovered Eepock right behind him. "Hug Boy, you need to go...go to Kingdom Falls and help your mom! Your mom is hurt. Look...I know what I said before. But this time, it's different and you can help. Now go!" In fear Hug said, " What about the cats?" Big tears filled his big brown eyes as he asked the question. Eepock replied in a deep, gruff voice. "Boy, leave the cats to me!" Then he YELLED, "MOVE IT BOY! NOW GO...HURRY! Hug, GO help your mom!"

Hug quickly sped off and ran as fast as he could toward Kingdom Falls. He had to save his mom and nothing else mattered. He ran hard for a long time until he spotted Sam sitting in a tree. Hug skidded on the wet surface and finally stopped. Excitedly and panting Hug said, "Sam, it's my mom! I need your help! Have you seen her?"

"WHOOO" exclaimed Sam, THE OLD OWL.

Anxiously Hug replied, "Dang it Sam...It's my mom! Eepock said my mom is hurt and I need to find her! I need your help...And the cats may...Where is my mom? Eepock said you..."

Sam interrupted. "WHOOO Boy! Stop jabbering! I'm trying to tell you something, if you'll let me get a word in edgewise!" He blinked his big yellow eyes twice, lifted one wing, pointed and said, "Go toward the large oak tree ahead. Beyond it, find the large rock. Your mom lies near it. Boy, you must hurry! The cats have gathered nearby!" Sam opened both large wings, flapped once and SWISH, he was gone. Hug took off and ran until he passed the big oak tree, then, he spotted the big rock. Near it, just as Sam had described, Hug saw his mom. He rushed to her side, nudged her and tried to wake her up. Mrs. Brown moaned slightly. Hug nudged her again and gently tried to coax her up. She was weak and dizzy from the fall. He nudged her several more times until, finally, she stood up. Neither one of them were aware of the danger that quietly approached!

The cats had gathered in a thicket near the base of the falls. Not only did they have one live target in sight, they had two! The cats watched for a moment, then, crouched low to the ground and slowly inched closer. The rain and heavy underbrush helped to hide their advance. The big cats setup to attack!

Suddenly the sound of a big SPLASH came from the river, followed by a loud blood-curdling GROWL and then, a nasty HISS! Immediately, the cats stopped. Eepock the Croc showed himself, all 2,000 pounds of him. He moved between the cats and the big rock where Mrs. Brown and Hug stood. Then, he echoed another loud GROWL and HISS that made the cats' fur frizz up. The cats were startled and scared, so, their slow advance changed to a slow retreat. They backed up to the edge of the woods and watched from the tall grass. One big cat did not retreat and stood his ground. IT WAS ZEPHER!

Quickly, Eepock turned his head toward Hug and in a gruff voice YELLED, "HUG Boy, get your mom into the river, NOW! Hurry up and Go! GO NOW!" Suddenly, Eepock's eyes turned from green to red as he changed from protect to attack mode!

Hug forcibly pushed Mrs. Brown toward the river as hard as he could push. Finally, SPLASH! Hug pushed her toward the center of the Winding River as the strong current quickly grabbed and carried them downstream and out of danger.

After a loud ROAR, Zepher rushed Eepock and managed to put a gash into his side with his claws! Zepher charged back and forth, each time looking for the opportunity to make the final, fatal bite! During the battle, Eepock had moved closer to the river's edge. Zepher saw his opening, charged in to make the fatal bite and leaped toward Eepock. Suddenly, Zepher was in mid air above Eepock with his mouth wide open and claws fully extended. Quickly, Eepock flipped his big tail, uncoiled like a snake, lunged and caught Zepher between his huge jaws as he came down.

With Zepher trapped, claws flying, Eepock slowly backed into the river and sank into it with a WHOOSH! A whirlpool formed as they sank. The other cats watched.

At Kingdom Falls, the water gushed, fell and exploded on the large boulders below as the thunderstorm moved off into the distance and took its fury with it. Faintly, its rumblings could still be heard in the distance.

SPLASH! GROWL! Eepock growled again as he came out of the river, moved up the bank and looked for another fight. Eepock had drowned Zepher. The other tigers and panthers had watched from the tall grass. Finally, they showed themselves, sat down near the edge of the woods and licked their paws; a gesture intended for Eepock and meant that they all extended their highest respect toward him.

Fabree walked from the group and said, "Eepock, I come in peace and I must thank you. If Zepher had lived, he would have forced his evil ways on the rest of us and I would be dead. He would have killed me for running away from Mt. Xcaber...the very same day he planned to kill you. Eepock, I owe you my life. And now, I can go back to my mate. I just came to say that." Respectfully, Fabree slowly turned and walked away.

Eepock watched Fabree for a moment as his soft side kicked in. He called out to her and said, "Fabree, glad you are safe. I'm glad there's at least one in this whole darn place who knows how to show gratitude!" Eepock mumbled to himself, walked toward the river, slide into it and disappeared with a SPLASH!

BOOK 4 - CONTINUATION

CHAPTER 2: HUG THE HERO

The big thunder, rain and lightning storm had lasted for all night and ended as quickly as it came. The rain had stopped and only hushed rumblings of the thunder could be heard off in the distance. Puddles of water were on the ground everywhere as dawn broke and cast its glow over the plains. White fluffy clouds replaced the black clouds and vibrant colors of gold, pink and orange glowed across the morning sky. Many animals gathered near the river in front of Grassy Knolls where everyone became saddened to think they had lost two of their members. They stood in silence. Suddenly, the silence broke when Holly YELLED, "LOOK! Look at the river! Mom and Hug! They are OKAY!"

All Rivers' Pond community gathered together as Sam, the old owl, watched from a large branch of a nearby tree. They couldn't believe their eyes! For the first time, they saw Hug without a coat of mud and, they soon realized he did not stink. All of Rivers' Pond community admired Hug for his courage and respected him for it. They were very surprised when they found out that Eepock had stood up against the cats at Kingdom Falls to protect Hug and Mrs. Brown.

Hug came out of the Winding River with Mrs. Brown at his side. As they did, Hug looked back toward the river and saw Eepock with his big green eyes glowing. With a soft adoring voice Hug said, "Eepock, thank you. I hope to see you again...my friend."

Eepock, in his usual gruff voice retorted, "DON'T count on it!" [GROWLED] Then, he rushed into the Winding River with a SPLASH, climbed out onto the opposite bank and mumbled. "Young whippersnappers...don't know anything! See me again? YEAH! See me again next time when needs help. That's when!

"OHHH...and there will DEFINITELY be a next time!" Eepock mumbled and advanced to the river.

Eepock found a nice sandy spot along the shore of the Winding River and plopped down on it. After the all-night ordeal, he was very, very tired. Sleepily, Eepock said, "Oh, a friend huh?" He opened his mouth very wide, yawned and softly said, "Hug boy...a good boy. Oh, I need a nap, harrumph." [Nub Nub Nub] [Zzzzzzzz] Eepock fell fast to sleep.

On the opposite shore, everybody had congregated into a large circle around Hug and Mrs. Brown. Simon and Holly entered the circle and went toward the center of it to greet Hug and their mom. While everyone looked on, Simon nudged his nose behind Hug's ear and said, "Huga Huga Hippo." And for the first time, Holly did the same. The low murmur turned into loud praises of excitement. Everyone was so happy that Hug and Mrs. Brown returned home safely.

Hug Brown was honored by all of the Rivers' Pond community for his courageous deeds. They all praised him for his respectful change. Hug became a hero and, this time, he was tagged with a very different, special name. It was a very special name that his little brother Simon, knew only...too well.

"Huga Huga Hippo" they called him! A shy young hippo who once was a shameful brown blob. Now, Hug was a true shining star who had proved real courage, honor, respect and affection toward his family and to the rest of Rivers' Pond community. Hug will remain a hero and an inspiration to everyone. Forever!

THE END

BRENDA C. MERCHANT

In 1959, Brenda was about eleven when her family moved to Alaska. They lived in both

Cooper Landing and Anchorage prior to acquiring a homestead in Willow. Brenda graduated from Wasilla High School in 1967. In 2000, she acquired an Associate of Science degree from the University of Alaska - Anchorage. She held technical positions within the Electric and Telephone industries where writing skills were utilized with regard to specialized contracts. In late 2009, Brenda launched her own publishing company and published *Poems By A Country Girl* written by Evelyn J Satterfield-Johnson, a friend of the family. In February and April of 2010, the Alaska Writers Guild presented her with both third and first place certificates for great writing in non-fiction and fiction, respectively.

In 2010, *Huga Huga Hippo* was both authored and published by Brenda C Merchant dba A-Gator Publishing.

With a dynamic history and an energized outlook, Brenda embarks upon a new adventure as a self-publisher and author in her retirement.

"I've always had lots of energy, a huge imagination, faith in mankind and a passion for writing. As for writing, time and opportunity were hard to find while raising my children and working fulltime. My goal is to retire soon. Afterward, I'd like to write often and fulfill the nagging urge. Besides, I like new adventures. In retirement, I will enjoy family and friends, learn to write many things and, by the Grace of God, will continue to have the ability to follow my dreams wherever they may lead!"

Books inspired by my grandsons Corbin & Caleb Merchant

CPSIA information can be obtained
at www.ICGtesting.com
Printed in the USA
BVHW020901150419
545533BV00003B/40/P

9 781796 026467